Dom's day out!

Om KIDZ
An imprint of Om Books International

Om Kidz | Om Books International

Reprinted in 2023

Corporate & Editorial Office
A-12, Sector 64, Noida 201 301
Uttar Pradesh, India
Phone: +91 120 477 4100
Email: editorial@ombooks.com
Website: www.ombooksinternational.com

Sales Office
107, Ansari Road, Darya Ganj
New Delhi 110 002, India
Phone: +91 11 4000 9000
Email: sales@ombooks.com
Website: www.ombooks.com

ISBN: 978-93-52760-23-7

Printed in India

10 9 8 7 6 5 4 3 2

Dom's day out!

Paste your photograph here

My name is

Dom, the **duck** is bored of working at his **desk**. He takes a **day** off.

He goes for a walk with his friend **Dodo,** the **dog**. **Dodo digs** up mud.

Dom and **Dodo** both get **dirty**.

They go for a **dip** in the **deep** pool.

Dom and **Dodo** shake a bit to **dry** off. Soon, they are good to go.

All of a sudden, they hear music.
Dom and **Dodo** follow the music.
It is coming from a house.

It is **Daisy,** the **donkey's** house. They see her **dancing.** **Dom** and **Dodo** join her.

Dom, **Dodo** and **Daisy dance** all **day**. Soon, they **decide** it is time to leave.

Dom and **Dodo** invite **Daisy** to their home. They all have a nice **dinner** together.

After **dinner**, **Dodo** wants
to eat something sweet.
So they eat **donuts**.

Daisy does not like **donuts**. **Dom** offers her a plate of **dates**. **Daisy** eats them.

Soon, it is **dark**. It is time for **Daisy** to go home.

Dom and **Dodo** wish **Daisy** a good night and sweet **dreams**.

Soon, **Dodo** goes home as well.

Dom wishes him good night.

They all have had a very nice **day**.

Know your words

Naming words

Dom	dog	donuts
duck	donkey	dates
desk	Daisy	
Dodo	dinner	

Describing words

dirty	dark	dry
deep		

Doing words

dig	decide	dreams
dip	dance	

Sight words

day	does	do

Colour the drops with words starting with the letter ‘**Dd**’.

swim

day

desk

cold

stream

dance

deep

donkey

soon

dog

Change the first letter in the given words to make a new word.

Dog = ___og

Deep = ___eep

Day = ___ay

Down = ___own

Do = ___o

Duck = ___uck

Match the following words beginning with the letter '**Dd**' with their images.

desk • • 

day • • 

Dom • • 

door • •